A FA
for CASEY

written by Cindy Rogers
pictures by Davy Jones

STANDARD
PUBLISHING
Cincinnati, Ohio

"My God will . . . give you everything you need."
Philippians 4:19

The Standard Publishing Company, Cincinnati, Ohio
A division of Standex International Corporation
© 1995 by The Standard Publishing Company
All rights reserved.
Printed in the United States of America.
02 01 00 99 98 97 96 95   5 4 3 2 1

Library of Congress Catalog Card Number 94-067877
ISBN 0-7847-0301-9

Scripture from the *International Children's Bible,* New Century Version.
© 1986, 1989 by Word Publishing, Dallas, Texas 75039. Used by permission.

Edited by Diane Stortz
Designed by Coleen Davis

Contents

Aunt Amanda

Casey lay in the front yard
on a hot summer day.
"Mom," he said,
"will our family always be
just you and me?"

"Maybe," said his mother.

She was digging a deep hole.

"Well," said Casey,

"I need a sister for my birthday."

Boomer barked and

stuck his nose

in the dirt.

Casey's mother pounded a post
into the hole.
She nailed a new mailbox
on the post.
"Maybe Sara can come over
to play tomorrow," she said.
"And I have a surprise.
Aunt Amanda is coming
for a visit."
Casey jumped up.
He loved Aunt Amanda.
Boomer wagged his shaggy tail.

Aunt Amanda arrived by bus

from New Mexico.

She was an artist.

She had boxes and boxes

of paints and brushes and paper.

"Casey, help me decide

what to paint today," she said.

Casey and Boomer

loved to paint

with Aunt Amanda.

Aunt Amanda stayed a week.

Then she got back on the bus

and went home to New Mexico.

Casey could not think

of anything to paint.

"Will she come again soon?"

he asked.

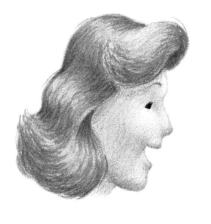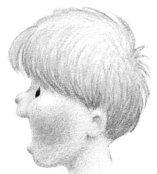

Casey's mother shook her head.

"Not for a while," she said.

"But Uncle Stanford is coming

from Montana."

"He is?" yelled Casey.

Uncle Stanford

had a very big laugh.

And he wrote mystery stories.

Casey could hardly wait.

Uncle Stanford

Casey and his mother

met Uncle Stanford at the airport.

"Hey, Uncle Stanford!"

shouted Casey.

Uncle Stanford laughed and said,

"I need to solve the mystery

of the missing suitcase."

Uncle Stanford stayed a week.

He and Casey found

the missing suitcase.

They read *all* of Casey's

favorite books.

And they wrote a story

about Boomer.

Then Uncle Stanford got back

on the airplane

and went home to Montana.

Casey could not look

at the airplane as it flew away.

"Mom, can we live in Montana
with Uncle Stanford?"
asked Casey on the way home.
"No," said his mother.
"But you can write to him."

In the grocery store, Casey asked,

"Can we go to New Mexico

and live with Aunt Amanda?"

"No," said his mother.

"But you can call her

on the phone."

At the veterinarian's,

waiting for Boomer's shot,

Casey asked,

"Can we go to Minnesota to live

with Grandpa and Grandma?"

"No," said his mother.

"*But* — they are coming

for a visit very soon!"

"Really?" shouted Casey.

Grandpa Tilford told stories

about Norway and trolls.

Grandma Leona played songs

on her little organ.

Casey hugged the cat

sitting next to him.

He could hardly wait!

19

Grandma and Grandpa

The big green car from Minnesota
finally arrived.

Grandpa Tilford

and Grandma Leona brought

the little
organ,

a birdhouse,

and bags of new apples.

Casey and Boomer

helped Grandpa

set up the birdhouse.

They listened to his stories.

They helped Grandma

make apple pies and applesauce.

They sang along

when Grandma played the organ.

It was a great week.

Then Grandpa and Grandma
got back in the big green car.
They smiled and waved good-bye.
Casey waved, but he didn't smile.
Boomer howled.

"I . . . I wish *everyone*
didn't live so far away!"
Casey said at dinner.

25

Casey's mother hugged him.

"Once, a long time ago,"

she said,

"God wanted a bigger family, too.

So he made one . . .

a whole world full.

Maybe you can find a way

to make one, too."

Casey talked to God about it.

"Help me make a bigger family,

like you did," he prayed.

And God gave him an idea.

Casey's Idea

The next morning,

Casey knocked on Sara's door.

"Will you be my sister?"

Casey asked Sara.

"I already *am* a sister," said Sara.

"But my baby brother cries a lot.

So I will be *your* sister."

Casey and Sara drew chalk
dinosaurs on the sidewalk.
They gave Boomer a bath.
Then they rested
under the oak tree.

When Casey's mother

went to work,

Casey went to Melba's house.

Melba was his baby-sitter.

She always had wonderful ideas.

Like parades!

Bang! Cling! Clang!

went the drum and spoon

and can.

Scrape! Ding! Rattle!

went the sticks and bell

and shaker.

It was great fun!

30

"Melba, will you be my aunt?"

asked Casey.

"My real aunt lives far away.

But you are fun like she is."

"I would love to be your aunt,"

said Melba.

And they beat the drum wildly.

Mr. Burleyman was Casey's
Sunday school teacher.
Every Sunday,
he gave Casey a big hug.
That night, Casey and Boomer
called Mr. Burleyman
on the phone.

"Mr. Burleyman," said Casey,

"I need an uncle.

My real uncle lives far away.

Would you be my uncle?"

"Sounds like fun,"

said Mr. Burleyman.

"Does this mean two hugs

on Sundays?"

"Yes!" said Casey.

He knew he would feel squished.

"Then I will be your uncle,"

said Mr. Burleyman.

35

More New Family

The next day,

Casey and Boomer ran

to Mr. Pettibone's yard.

Casey liked Mr. Pettibone.

He let Casey dig in his garden

and pick his strawberries.

He even let Casey lick

the cake bowl in his kitchen.

36

"I have something important
to ask you," said Casey.
"Then we need
to have milk and
cupcakes," said
Mr. Pettibone.
"Let's go inside."

"Do you have a grandson?"

Casey asked Mr. Pettibone.

"Yes, I do, but he lives far away,"

said Mr. Pettibone.

"I live far away from my grandpa,

too," said Casey.

"So will you be my grandpa

here at home?"

38

"A splendid idea!"

said Mr. Pettibone.

"Let's celebrate!"

He put candles in their cupcakes.

He even gave

a cupcake

to Boomer.

On Saturday, Casey went to work
with his mother.
He visited Ms. Pinkton.
She was his mother's boss.
Ms. Pinkton let Casey
type on her computer.
She even gave him chocolate
from her candy jar.

"Ms. Pinkton," said Casey,

"can I be your grandson?"

Ms. Pinkton thought about it.

She had no grandchildren

of her own.

"Good idea, Casey!

We will make a contract."

Ms. Pinkton turned on
her computer. She typed,
"I, Ms. Pinkton, and you, Casey,
shall be grandmother
and grandson."
Casey pushed
"Print."

Then Casey signed his name
on the paper.

Ms. Pinkton signed her name.

They made a copy
at the copy machine.

They each kept one.

Happy Birthday, Casey

The week of his birthday,

Casey got lots of mail

from his family far away . . .

. . . from Aunt Amanda

in New Mexico . . .

. . . from Uncle Stanford

in Montana . . .

and from Grandma Leona

and Grandpa Tilford

in Minnesota.

But at his birthday supper,

Casey had lots of family, too,

. . . his mother and Boomer . . .

. . . Sara . . .

Melba . . .

. . . Mr. Burleyman . . .

. . . Mr. Pettibone

. . . and Ms. Pinkton.

It was wonderful fun!

And that night, Casey prayed,
"Thank you, God,
for my new family.
Now, please help me find
a bigger family for Boomer!"